MW00891837

Love, Emily
and Scarlet

STRETCH LIKE SCARLET
First Edition

Published by Friendly City Books, Columbus, Mississippi
Text © 2020 by Emily Liner
Illustrations © 2020 by John Clark IV
All rights reserved.

No part of this publication may be reproduced or stored in a retrieval system or transmitted in any form or by any means electronic, mechanical, photocopying, recording, or otherwise without written permission of the publisher.

For information regarding permission, please email **info@friendlycitybooks.com** or visit **stretchlikescarlet.com**.

Library of Congress Control Number: 2020915509
ISBN: 978-0-578-74605-0

Written in Hancock County, Mississippi
Illustrated in New Orleans, Louisiana
Printed in Canada by Friesens Corporation
First Printing, September 2020

STRETCH
LIKE SCARLET

Written by
EMILY LINER

Illustrated by
JOHN CLARK IV

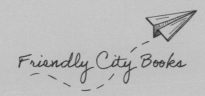

Friendly City Books

I start off the day
curled up in a ball
under the covers
because I'm so small.

"Hey Scarlet, wake up!"
My ears perk up tall.

But first,
a good
stretch!
It's the best
thing of all.

I **pull back** on my paws
and let out a **yawn**

Then I **push forward**
to welcome the dawn.

I
**lift
up my
chin**
to make my
neck long.

Stretching is great for when I need to **scratch**

or when there's a friend
running by me to **catch.**

I see if
you're watching
and **beg**
for a pat.

I **crawl** on my belly

and **roll** on my back.

Look at me **stand up**
on my tippy toes—

I can get them to **touch**
all the way to my nose.

I can **jump** up so high

and **wiggle** down low.

When it's time for a **walk** I'll be ready to go!

Now I'm warmed up
for a **shake** and a **twist**.

SCARLET

Emily adopted Scarlet in 2017--but Scarlet won't tell her how old she is. The inseparable duo enjoy reading with kids and seniors with People Animals Love, Inc., a 501(c)3 nonprofit organization based in Washington, DC. 5% of the profits from sales of this book are donated to PAL.

Learn more at peopleanimalslove.org.

EMILY LINER
Author

Emily is the founder of Friendly City Books in Columbus, Mississippi. She is a graduate of Georgetown University and received an MBA from the University of North Carolina. This book is dedicated to her grandmother and namesake, who makes a cameo in these pages, and her mother, who inspired her love of reading and encouraged her new business venture.

JOHN CLARK IV
Illustrator

John is an illustrator and designer in New Orleans, Louisiana. He is the founder of HOP & JAUNT Creative Agency. The artwork in this book is dedicated to his niece Reagan who loves stories and has a terrific imagination.